MW00477928

Baby Screams Miracle

Clare Barron

A SAMUEL FRENCH ACTING EDITION

SAMUEL FRENCH

FOUNDED 1830

SAMUELFRENCH.COM
SAMUELFRENCH-LONDON.CO.UK

FOR PRODUCTION ENQUIRIES

UNITED STATES AND CANADA
Info@SamuelFrench.com
1-866-598-8449

UNITED KINGDOM AND EUROPE
Plays@SamuelFrench-London.co.uk
020-7255-4302

Each title is subject to availability from Samuel French, depending upon country of performance. Please be aware that BABY SCREAMS MIRACLE may not be licensed by Samuel French in your territory. Professional and amateur producers should contact the nearest Samuel French office or licensing partner to verify availability.

MUSIC USE NOTE

Licensees are solely responsible for obtaining formal written permission from copyright owners to use copyrighted music in the performance of this play and are strongly cautioned to do so. If no such permission is obtained by the licensee, then the licensee must use only original music that the licensee owns and controls. Licensees are solely responsible and liable for all music clearances and shall indemnify the copyright owners of the play(s) and their licensing agent, Samuel French, against any costs, expenses, losses and liabilities arising from the use of music by licensees. Please contact the appropriate music licensing authority in your territory for the rights to any incidental music.

IMPORTANT BILLING AND CREDIT REQUIREMENTS

If you have obtained performance rights to this title, please refer to your licensing agreement for important billing and credit requirements.

BABY SCREAMS MIRACLE was first produced by Clubbed Thumb at The Wild Project in New York City on May 24, 2014. The performance was directed by Portia Krieger, with sets by Daniel Zimmerman, costumes by Sarah Laux, lights by Derek Wright, sound by Brandon Wolcott, and projections by Bart Cortright. The Production Manager was Cody Westgaard and the Stage Manager was Lisa McGinn. The cast was as follows:

CYNTHIA . . . . Susannah Flood

KAYDEN . . . . Ismenia Mendes

BARBARA . . . . Caitlin O'Connell

CAROL . . . . Danielle Skraastad

GABRIEL . . . . Danny Wolohan

CHARACTERS

BARBARA – Mother of Carol, late 60s
CAROL – Mother of Cynthia and Kayden, early 40s
GABRIEL – Father of Cynthia and Kayden, early 40s
CYNTHIA – 26
KAYDEN – 5

SETTING

Eureka, Washington. A small town along the Columbia River Gorge.

A NOTE ON THE SET

The house becomes less and less livable throughout the course of the storm. First the living room is gone then the bedrooms… The bathroom is a final refuge (isn't it always?) It's helpful to think of the world shrinking, shrinking, shrinking until it explodes into the huge expanse of the open field and forest. Daniel Zimmerman designed a brilliant set where furniture was overturned as the storm raged on. We called this "the pile" (and it's referenced as such in the script). Ultimately the upside-down and every-which-way furniture stood in for the hills, logs and rocks of the forest. The bathtub became the car. In the final scene of the play – when we snap back to the house – all that was needed was a light shift and suddenly the bed was just a bed again, the tub just a tub.

NOTE ON EVERYTHING ELSE

All the religious language and impulses of these people should be treated with compassion and respect.

The play wants to be as bloody and violent and spectacular as possible (i.e., a tree coming through the roof). But its soul is lo-fi.

A slash (/) indicates an interruption in speech.

SPECIAL THANKS

A very special thank you to…

The goddess Maria Striar who taught me how to revise a play and is an incredible advocate for new voices in NYC. Portia Krieger and her exquisite, wild production. Our incredible team of actors, designers and crew. Tom Lehman who let me write this on the floor of his bathroom and forgave me for abandoning him during his knee surgery because I was in Tech. Nora DeVeau-Rosen. Michael Bulger. Youngblood. Colleen Sullivan. David Herskovits. Eyad Houssami. Rachel Viola. And of course: 303 Douglass (Borinsky, Hardy, Hill). And my crazy Barron family.

For Sparpe

Night. The master bedroom. Gabriel is curled up in bed. Carol appears in the doorway. She is visibly pregnant.

CAROL. Are you ready?

GABRIEL. Just waiting for you

CAROL. On the bed?

GABRIEL. I thought it'd be cozy

CAROL. I might fall asleep

GABRIEL. Let's pull up a chair

CAROL. Okay

GABRIEL. Hi

CAROL. Hi

He takes her hands and looks into her eyes.

GABRIEL. I love you

CAROL. Are you going to look at me like that the whole time?

GABRIEL. No. Why? I'll probably shut my eyes

CAROL. If you look at me like that I'll laugh I can't help it

GABRIEL. You can laugh if you want to. Laughter is a blessing

CAROL. I know. I know it is. I laugh all the time.

GABRIEL. I know you do

Carol takes a deep breath.

GABRIEL. Oh. Are we breathing?

CAROL. I think it's nice to start with breathing

GABRIEL. Should I– ?

CAROL. If you want to, it'd be nice if you joined me

They take several deep breaths together, still holding hands. Finally…

GABRIEL. I thank you so much for Carol, Jesus. I love her so much. I thank you for the day that we were married. I ask you to bless Carol. And everything she puts her hand to. I ask that you help me to die to myself, Jesus, so that I can love Carol. In little ways, just *die* to myself. So that I can make her feel loved.

CAROL. Um. I thank you for my husband. I thank you for Gabriel, Jesus. I thank you for all the awesome things we've done together. *(long pause, then to Gabriel)* Let's just keep passing it back and forth.

GABRIEL. Okay. *(He clears his throat.)* I was mean today, Jesus. Why was I so mean? I hurt someone. I made him feel stupid when he didn't do anything wrong. I was feeling sorry for myself. And I took it out on him, Jesus, because he couldn't read my mind. Help me make it up to him. Help me to go out of my way to be kind to him tomorrow.

CAROL. We should pray for JD Burr who has cancer. Of the– Um. Pancreas. Pancreatic cancer. It's awful. I hear it's awful. And it's pulling Mandy apart. So if there's a miracle available… They deserve it. I really don't want him to die.

GABRIEL. Help me to be   **CAROL.** I thank you for

CAROL. Oh sorry

GABRIEL. No go ahead

CAROL. I'm done

GABRIEL. I just wanted to say: Help me be a life giver, and not a life taker, Lord Jesus. Help me to shed your light on my family.

    Silence.

CAROL. Also. Forgive us our sins, Lord.

GABRIEL. Yes

CAROL. I know we are wicked…cruel…selfish…lazy… ungrateful…blind…

I used to spend a lot of energy hating myself. I thought I was evil. Everything I said was bad. When I went out with my friends, I'd come home and spend the entire next day wallowing in the shame of all the mean-spirited things I'd said the night before. It was…unproductive. And also egocentric.

    The sound of moaning.

GABRIEL. Honey

CAROL. It *is* egocentric. But now I understand that I'm *okay*

GABRIEL. Carol

CAROL. Now I understand that I'm doing *great.* Right now. This instant. Just sitting here. I'm on the right track, Jesus. Even though I'm awful. I'm perfect. Even though I'm pathetic–

GABRIEL. Carol? Honey? The freezer is still moaning

CAROL. It is?

GABRIEL. Did you replace the evaporator / thing?

CAROL. Oh, shit. I forgot

GABRIEL. God dammit, Carol

CAROL. I thought about it today and so I thought I'd done it because I'd thought about it.

GABRIEL. I asked you two days ago

CAROL. I know

GABRIEL. What did you do all day?

CAROL. I'll just– I'll just go do that icebox tappy thing-y. That usually makes it stop

GABRIEL. No, no. You stay. You stay in that. Whatever you were in just a second ago. You stay in that and meditate and I'll be right back.

CAROL. Hurry, honey. It's going to wake Kayden.

    Gabriel exits. The moaning continues.

CAROL. Gabriel, honey? Would you bring me some tea? Um.

    Carol spies a mug of old coffee across the room. She goes to it and takes a sip. Spits it out. Takes another sip.

CAROL. Bedtime! Bedtime, Carol! Bad! Bad!

This cup of coffee makes me feel so good, Jesus

It makes me feel like I'm in love with life

It saves me, Jesus

When I am crippled with self-loathing and depression

It lifts me out of my funk and makes me feel like LIFE today is still possible

It gives me the courage to respond to my emails and not feel ashamed

But sometimes the high is too good, Jesus

Sometimes the high leaves me staring out the window just thinking of all the people I've met and all the people I love and all the people I could write emails to…

And then I just sit there, feeling euphoric, and I don't get anything done

And afterwards, the high is gone and I'm all alone with no sense of accomplishment

Help me, Jesus, know how to lift my spirits without chemicals

It's just a cup of coffee, Jesus

Don't let it control my life

> *She takes a sip, puts the coffee down and crawls into bed.*

CAROL. GABE? NOT CHAMOMILE

GABRIEL. *(off)* I ALREADY POURED IT

CAROL. IT'S OKAY. NEVER MIND

GABRIEL. DO YOU WANT ME TO POUR YOU ANOTHER CUP?

CAROL. NO

GABRIEL. IT'S NOT A PROBLEM. WE'VE GOT PLENTY OF HOT WATER

CAROL. PLEASE DON'T POUR ME ANOTHER CUP

> *Gabriel enters with two cups of tea.*

GABRIEL. I'm sorry I already poured it

CAROL. It's okay. It just tastes like soap bubbles to me

GABRIEL. I know that, I just forgot. I should've remembered.

> *He hands her the tea.*

CAROL. You are an angel

GABRIEL. Hot

> *She blows on it and puts it down on her bedside table.*

GABRIEL. Carol?

CAROL. Yes

GABRIEL. Would you forgive me for my harsh words just now?

CAROL. I forgive you

GABRIEL. I know you have a lot on your plate. And you didn't forget on purpose. Do you want to keep going?

CAROL. Sure

> *She yawns, lies back and closes her eyes.*

CAROL. Let's see. Jesus Jesus, thank you...
It's cold, isn't it? Do you think it's cold? It's really cold.

GABRIEL. The wind is up

CAROL. I'm chilly. I'm really cold

GABRIEL. Should I hold you?

CAROL. No, no. The sheets will be warm in a second

> *Gabriel gets into bed and holds her.*

GABRIEL. Well. I guess we should pray for all the people who might be cold tonight, Jesus

CAROL. The cats and the dogs

GABRIEL. The cats and the dogs

CAROL. And the deer

GABRIEL. And the deer too. And the people who don't have homes to go to. Watch over them, Jesus. And be with them tonight.
And we pray, Jesus. That you help bring our beautiful daughter Kayden out of her shell. That you help her

to grow up to be a happy, healthy, brave, strong little woman. And that you comfort her when she is sad and we can't reach her.

And we pray, Jesus. That if we should die tonight. Or if we should die tomorrow. You'll accept our souls as living members of your eternal kingdom. For now. And forever. Amen.

CAROL. Amen. *(pause)* Gabe?

GABRIEL. Uh-huh

CAROL. I don't like it when you talk like that

GABRIEL. Like what?

CAROL. When you say that you want to *die* so that you can love me, I don't like that

GABRIEL. It's a nice thing. It's a way for me to say how much I love you

CAROL. You sound like a creep

GABRIEL. Well, I don't have to say that anymore. If it upsets you I–

CAROL. It doesn't upset me, it creeps me out

GABRIEL. Well, I won't say it then. I'll just say it when I'm alone.

CAROL. Thank you

GABRIEL. No problem. Carol?

CAROL. Yes

GABRIEL. Aren't you going to drink your tea?

CAROL. I just like having it right here beside me

GABRIEL. You should drink it. It'll warm you up

CAROL. It is. It is warming me up

GABRIEL. Carol?

CAROL. Shhh sleeping

> *Gabriel turns off the light.*

———————

Night. The sound of the freezer moaning. Then wind. It builds until it is a massive storm. Hurricane-level winds. The sounds of things cracking, shifting, shattering, flying. Trees fall. A dog howls. People screaming, praying. The freezer door swings open and white light spills out into the kitchen.

Kayden sits up in bed in the dark. We can make out the white of the sheet, her nightgown, her eyeballs.

The wind stops. Morning. Kayden runs downstairs. She opens the front door and takes a step outside.

KAYDEN. All the trees fell down

———————————

Later that day in the living room. The front windows have blown out. There is broken glass everywhere. A pine tree has fallen halfway into the room.

Barbara sits in an armchair. Kayden lies on the carpet at her feet. Barbara lifts one of her feet and gently caresses Kayden with it – tickling her ribs and stroking her hair. A tropical breeze blows into the living room, mussing Barbara's hair and exposing her pink scalp.

Down the hall is a bathroom. The door to the bathroom has been blown off. The bathroom window is broken. Pine boughs litter the floor. Shampoos and conditioners are everywhere. Carol and Cynthia clean it up – ferrying trash bags and boxes to the hallway.

Like Carol, Cynthia is visibly pregnant. She has a prosthetic left foot.

On the bathroom mirror, in red lipstick, are the words: YOU ARE GORGEOUS. Below – in orange lipstick and a softer script – are the words: GEE THANKS

CYNTHIA. I thought you guys *died*

CAROL. It was just a bit of wind

CYNTHIA. I was picturing you all crushed and *dead.* I was literally *hysterical*

CAROL. We didn't die. We didn't even come close to dying. Gabriel slept right through it

CYNTHIA. You should go out there. Take a look around. Everyone's face is just covered in blood. / It's wild

CAROL. Oh come on now that is disgusting

CYNTHIA. From the broken glass! I'm serious! And some kid down the street got decapitated / by a tree branch

CAROL. Cynthia Stop

CYNTHIA. What?

CAROL. Are you joking with me?

CYNTHIA. I'm not joking. *Jesus.*

CAROL. Well. Geez. It was a weird storm.

CYNTHIA. Can I have this?

CAROL. What is it?

CYNTHIA. Scrunchy

CAROL. You'll have to ask Kayden. She's inherited all the scrunchies in this house.

CYNTHIA. It's my scrunchy

CAROL. Well then take it

Cynthia puts the scrunchy in her hair.

CYNTHIA. *(surveying the bathroom)* You have all these great cosmetics, Carol, and you never, ever use them

CAROL. I can't believe you're here

CYNTHIA. Is that okay?

CAROL. Of course

KAYDEN. MOM

CAROL. WHAT KAYDEN

KAYDEN. THERE'S AN EARTHWORM IN THE LIVING ROOM

CAROL. WELL TAKE IT OUTSIDE

> *Kayden picks up the worm. She carries it through the gaping holes where the windows should be and gingerly deposits it on the front patio.*

CAROL. She has to be told to do everything. It's exhausting

> *<<KABOOM>> Cynthia breaks one of Carol's compacts and powder goes everywhere. It's like a little explosion.*

CYNTHIA. Sorry, Mom

CAROL. It's fine

> *Carol goes back to cleaning the bathroom. Cynthia watches Carol. She reaches out to touch Carol's pregnant belly.*

CYNTHIA. I can't believe we're doing this together

CAROL. I know

CYNTHIA. Who would've predicted–

CAROL. It's nuts

CYNTHIA. It's insane

CAROL. It is absolutely nuts

CYNTHIA. It's a sign

CAROL. It's a miracle, that's what it is. God is a God of miracles. That's all I'm going to say.

CYNTHIA. You are absolutely huge

CAROL. I know

CYNTHIA. It is absolutely beautiful

CAROL. You look like me. It's creeping me out.

> *(beat)*

   Cynthia? Can you do me a favor?

CYNTHIA. Sure

CAROL. Can I ask you to pray with me? Just for a minute?

CYNTHIA. Oh. Um, sure.

> *They clasp hands and pray. Long silence.*

BARBARA. Did you put him in the dirt?

KAYDEN. What?

BARBARA. Did you put him in the dirt? You can't just leave
him on the concrete you've got to put him in the dirt

> *Kayden gets up and moves the worm so that he is
> in the dirt.*

BARBARA. You and your mother and your insects.

KAYDEN. What?

BARBARA. I said, "You and your mother and your insects."
One time your mother had a cold and I put her out on
the patio to warm her up. And she was looking up at
the sky with her mouth hanging open. And this little
blue butterfly comes and lands right on the tip of her
tongue. Inside her mouth. And I say to her, "Carol
Luanne, there is a butterfly on your tongue. Don't you
move." And she gives me this look – this extraordinary
look. Every inch of her is frozen still except these
bulging eyeballs coming at me sideways. And that
poor thing just starts to twitch. She's concentrating so
hard on staying still that she is twitching. And then she
sneezes

> *Barbara claps her hands.*

BARBARA. I was picking butterfly bits out of her teeth for
weeks

> *Long silence. Carol and Cynthia pray. Carol looks
> at Cynthia's prosthetic foot.*

CAROL. That's not your foot, is it?

CYNTHIA. It's my foot

CAROL. That is a fake foot

CYNTHIA. It's my new foot

CAROL. Are you kidding me?

CYNTHIA. No I'm–

CAROL. What happened to your foot?

CYNTHIA. Carol, I–

CAROL. We're sitting here talking for thirty-five minutes and you're not gonna even bring up the fact that you are walking around on a fake foot? Christ, Cynthia, last time I saw you, you had a flippin' foot

CYNTHIA. A computer fell on it

CAROL. What?

CYNTHIA. A computer monitor

CAROL. What?

CYNTHIA. At a trade show

CAROL. A monitor?

CYNTHIA. Really truly

CAROL. I didn't know that could happen

CYNTHIA. Me either. I was in shock when the doctor told me. I was literally in shock.

CAROL. I'm in shock! I'm in shock right now about your fake foot!

> *They are both laughing.*

CAROL. Well are you going to tell me how it happened?

CYNTHIA. I told you. A computer fell on it

CAROL. What does that *mean*

CYNTHIA. It means that a computer monitor on one of those rolly-thingies–

CAROL. A cart! A push cart!

CYNTHIA. Went flying off at a trade show and landed on my foot–

CAROL. Oh my God

CYNTHIA. And smashed all the bones in my foot–

CAROL. Oh dear Lord

CYNTHIA. And all the nerves–

CAROL. Oh my God, Cynthia

CYNTHIA. And at first they thought they could fix it, and then the doctor literally said he was going to have to amputate my foot. And I just looked at him like– Who on earth are you speaking to?

CAROL. And that was before or after you got pregnant?

CYNTHIA. Before. That was well before

CAROL. I thought I had some shit but hats off, Cynthia. Your shit takes the CAKE. Excuse my language, but your shit takes the cake

CYNTHIA. What's your shit, tell me about your shit

CAROL. Oh my god. I'm crying

CYNTHIA. Me too. I'm crying

CAROL. Oh Lord. This is too– This is

> *(Carol breathes.)*

You should stay. Hang out for awhile. I think it'd be good for us.

> *Gabriel enters the living room carrying water jugs and glow sticks. He is covered in blood.*

KAYDEN. MOM

CAROL. What?

KAYDEN. MOM

CAROL. What?

KAYDEN. DAD

GABRIEL. Don't go out there. I hit a deer

BARBARA. Oh my god, Gabriel

CAROL. *(calling from the bathroom)* IS THE DEER OKAY?

BARBARA. Oh my god, Carol, come out here. Just look at him.

> *Carol and Cynthia enter from the bathroom.*

CAROL. Jesus Christ. How fast were you driving?

GABRIEL. It went through the windshield. Pieces of it are still in the grill. I think I got everything out of the car. Except for the blood, which. We're going to have to get a professional cleaning service, I think. Or a new car.

BARBARA. I'm going to go look at the car

> *Barbara exits.*

GABRIEL. I was just trying to get home as fast as possible

CAROL. Poor baby deer

GABRIEL. Oh my god. Cynthia

CYNTHIA. Hi

GABRIEL. You're here

CYNTHIA. I saw the pictures on the news and all of a sudden I was driving over the mountains

GABRIEL. I didn't know you were coming

CAROL. Me either

> *Carol and Gabriel exchange a look.*

GABRIEL. Uh, wow. It's so good to see you.

BARBARA. *(off)* OH MY GOD. CAROL. YOU HAVE GOT TO COME OUT HERE. THERE IS A DEER-SIZED HOLE IN THE MIDDLE OF YOUR WINDSHIELD. AND ITS REAR END IS STILL… THERE ARE… EVERYTHING IS SPLATTERED. EVERYTHING IS JUST SPLATTERED

CAROL. Where is Kayden?

KAYDEN. I'm right here.

CAROL. Kayden don't go out there okay? Actually, would you do me a favor? Would you go sit in your special bathroom spot Aunt Cynthia showed you earlier?

KAYDEN. Hi Daddy

GABRIEL. Hi Angel

CAROL. Don't look at Daddy, Kayden. I don't want you to see him like this

BARBARA. CAROL. YOU HAVE GOT TO SEE THIS OH MY LORD. OH MY LORDY LORD

> *Kayden exits to the bathroom. Carol exits to the car.*

BARBARA. OH MY LORD

CAROL. OH MY *GAWD! GABRIEL!*

BARBARA. OH MY LORDY LORD

> *Silence. Cynthia and Gabriel alone in the living room.*

CYNTHIA. Hi

GABRIEL. Hi

CYNTHIA. It's really intense. Seeing you like this. Like all bloody and–

> *Carol and Barbara come back inside.*

CAROL. Well, congratulations, Big Stuff. That was truly the feat of a lifetime.

BARBARA. That is such an unusual deer collision. Never in my life have I– Once I heard of a falcon coming through a windshield up near Ephrata. Some kid with some sports car. But never a deer. Never a deer. Like *that.* A deer inside the car. Well, that is just strange. That is just too big to be inside a car. It's extreme times, isn't it? Everything is just more extreme than I remember it.

CAROL. Are you alright?

GABRIEL. I'm fine but

CAROL. What?

GABRIEL. Jedediah didn't make it.

He was in the back seat. The deer hit him. He just– I was going really fast. A deer is a big animal. Sharp, sharp animal. Sharp part of the animal. I'm sorry. I don't think he suffered.

CAROL. Where is Kayden?

CYNTHIA. She's in the bathroom

CAROL. Don't tell Kayden

CYNTHIA. How about I go be with Kayden.

> *Cynthia exits to the bathroom.*

BARBARA. Carol, honey, he had a good life. He was an old dog.

> *Carol walks up to Gabriel and hits him hard on the chest.*

CAROL. Stupid.

> *She hits him again.*

CAROL. Stupid.

GABRIEL. I'm sorry

BARBARA. What did you do with him?

GABRIEL. I dragged him and the deer out back. They're inside the little Wendy house for now

CAROL. You left them together!

GABRIEL. *For now.* I just didn't want other animals eating them while we were gone. Until we can properly... dispose–

CAROL. Bury him

GABRIEL. Until we can bury him. And you know. Give him a funeral. A nice funeral. I'll make him a coffin.

———————

Cynthia and Kayden in the wrecked bathroom.

CYNTHIA. What do you want to be when you grow up, Kayden?

KAYDEN. Um

CYNTHIA. If you could be anything in the world what would you be?

KAYDEN. I'd be First Lady

CYNTHIA. Well that's silly. Why would you want to be that? You should be the president. Don't you want to be the president?

KAYDEN. No

CYNTHIA. Did you know that all of the presidents of the United States before this president were girls?

KAYDEN. No

CYNTHIA. Kayden, come here. Do you know who I am?

KAYDEN. Aunt Cynthia

CYNTHIA. No, I'm your sister. Sister Cynthia. Because your mommy and daddy had me when they were very, very young. And then they didn't really want me like they wanted you, so. So you know what that means? That means you're a very lucky girl.

And that means you have a big sister. And right now, I know it feels like I'm more of a mommy than a sister, but one day we're gonna both be grown-ups and we're gonna talk about grown-up things and we'll be like sisters. I'm excited for that. I'm excited for that to happen.

Kayden looks at her.

CYNTHIA. Your mom and dad are pretty nice now huh?

Kayden nods.

CYNTHIA. That's good.

They don't yell at you or–

KAYDEN. Sometimes they yell

CYNTHIA. Well, yeah, sometimes they have to yell.

They take you to the park and the ice-skating rink…

KAYDEN. Dairy Queen

CYNTHIA. Oh yeah? That's good. That's cool.

They let you go to the bathroom whenever you need to?

KAYDEN. Yeah

CYNTHIA. That's good

Kayden looks at her.

CYNTHIA. You're very shy, do you know that? I think your mommy and daddy think there's something wrong with you but I just think you're shy and quiet. Do you think that's true?

KAYDEN. I don't know

CYNTHIA. You shouldn't be shy. Being shy doesn't get you very far in life. You have to put yourself out there, you know. You have to stand out. People say it's the shy, nerdy kids who come back and get revenge later in life, but they're wrong. It's the kids with charisma, you know what I'm saying? The homecoming queen. That's who you want to be. That's who dominates everyone else from the time she's born until the time she dies. It's true.

Come on. Let's practice. I say dance, you dance. Got it?
I say dance, you dance. Okay. Dance.

Kayden doesn't move.

CYNTHIA. You have to dance. You have to move. You have
to not be afraid to make a fool of yourself. Come on.
Dance. Dance. Dance, Kayden. Dance.

Kayden doesn't move.

CYNTHIA. Give me your shoes.

KAYDEN. What?

CYNTHIA. You didn't dance. Now you have to give me your
shoes.

*Kayden takes off her shoes and gives them to
Cynthia.*

CYNTHIA. Okay. Let's try this again. Dance. I want you to
dance. Come on. I don't care *how* you dance. I don't
care how well you dance. Just move. Just moooove, god
dammit. Do something.

Kayden doesn't move.

CYNTHIA. Give me your pants.

*Kayden takes off her pants and hands them to
Cynthia.*

CYNTHIA. I bet you feel pretty silly without your pants. And
it's cold outside. And another storm is coming soon.
And you're going to be without your shoes and without
your pants and who knows what else. So you better
dance, don't you think?

*Kayden bends at the knee a little bit – up and
down.*

CYNTHIA. Are you dancing? I can't tell. Is that dancing?

Gabriel enters.

GABRIEL. Oh, sorry. I'm looking for winter coats?

CYNTHIA. I have no idea

GABRIEL. Apparently there are winter coats somewhere in the bathroom?

No one knows.

GABRIEL. I'll just go ask Carol.

Gabriel exits. Cynthia and Kayden look at each other. Gabriel re-enters.

GABRIEL. Kayden, aren't you cold?

———————————

Carol and Barbara are in the living room, sweeping up broken glass. The storm gathers ominously in the background. Big black purple clouds moving in.

CAROL. You think the weather's getting worse?

BARBARA. The weather has been bad since the beginning of time. The weather was horrible at the beginning of time. I don't know why everyone says it's getting worse.

CAROL. I think it's getting worse

BARBARA. People just don't like change. So if this part of the world was a desert and that part of the world got tornadoes, and then the place with tornadoes becomes a desert, and the desert becomes a place with tornadoes, everybody feels worse off.

A lawn chair blows into the living room.

CAROL. Oh look

BARBARA. Oh look it's coming back

A big gust of wind.

BARBARA. Wheeeee

CAROL. It feels good. It feels like a spaceship is landing

The wind builds until it gets a little scary. It whips Carol's and Barbara's hair and steals a scarf from one of their necks.

CAROL. Stop it!

BARBARA. I command you to stop it!

CAROL. By the power vested in me I say STOP IT!

BARBARA. If you don't stop, this is what I'm gonna do:

I'm gonna take the clouds from the sky and turn them into a blanket. And then I'm gonna take the rain from the sky and use it to fill my warshing machine. And then I'm gonna get some electricity from the lightning and use it to power that warshing machine *and my dryer* and then I'm gonna warsh that blanket and dry it and I'll have a hot, dry blanket and you'll have nothing. No clouds, no rain, no lightning. Nothing.

> *Carol throws the lawn chair back out the window at the storm.*

> *Thunder, and then a huge gust of wind.*

CAROL. Oh my god! Trampoline! Trampoline! Oh my god!

> *A giant trampoline rolls into the living room. Carol and Barbara drop their brooms, run inside to safety and slam the door.*

———————

> *Calm. Cynthia is brushing her teeth in the blown-out bathroom. The window has been hastily boarded up. A little rain comes through one of the gaps.*

> *Gabriel enters. He wears a makeshift eye patch, and there is fresh blood on his face. It looks pretty gruesome.*

GABRIEL. Can I brush with you?

CYNTHIA. Sure. We can't spit. I mean, we can spit, but our toothpaste is just going to sit here in the sink

GABRIEL. Do you want me to get some water from the garage?

CYNTHIA. No, I think it's fine. Oh! But you need water for your toothbrush

GABRIEL. I'll just do it dry

> *They brush their teeth together, looking at each other in the mirror. They talk with toothbrushes in their mouths.*

CYNTHIA. Good job fixing the siding

GABRIEL. Thanks

CYNTHIA. That must've been scary. I'm sorry you got hurt.

> *He shrugs.*

GABRIEL. This is pretty awful [the toothbrush-ing]

CYNTHIA. You should've got some water

> *He shrugs.*

CYNTHIA. Um. I didn't flush the toilet

GABRIEL. Oh

CYNTHIA. I just didn't want you looking over there and noticing pee in the toilet

GABRIEL. Because of the

CYNTHIA. There's no water

GABRIEL. Right

CYNTHIA. I mean, actually, I don't usually flush the toilet. At home. When I just pee. But I mean, if I was in a stranger's house I would always flush the toilet. Just to be. You know. Respectful.

GABRIEL. Well I have to pee too so soon our pee will… co-mingle.

CYNTHIA. Ha ha

> *Cynthia spits.*

CYNTHIA. You could pee in the sink. Kill two birds with one stone.

GABRIEL. I could do that. But you'd have to leave first

CYNTHIA. What are you going to do if you have to poop?

GABRIEL. I was just wondering that myself

CYNTHIA. I'm so sorry to use that word in front of you–

GABRIEL. No, no it's a legitimate question–

CYNTHIA. I'd normally say shit but–

GABRIEL. I'd say the prudent thing to do is to dig a little hole out back near the pine trees

CYNTHIA. But it's raining

GABRIEL. It is raining

CYNTHIA. It's really raining hard

GABRIEL. And the taily-po will get us

CYNTHIA. Oh, yes. The taily-po

GABRIEL. The taily-po the taily-po I'm coming to get my taily-po

> *He lunges at her, tickling her ribs. She screams. He pulls her into a tight embrace.*

CAROL. *(off)* DID SOMEONE DIE UP THERE?

CYNTHIA. Uh-oh I guess we're in trouble

GABRIEL. We are in big, big trouble.

I'M MURDERING CYNTHIA! *(to Cynthia)* Are you smelling me? Don't smell me. There are deer guts. I haven't showered. Are you crying?

CYNTHIA. All day I've been waiting for someone to hug me but nobody did

GABRIEL. Oh honey

CYNTHIA. Just give me five more seconds

> *He holds her. Cynthia talks into Gabriel's sweater.*

CYNTHIA. Kayden's great.

GABRIEL. She is, isn't she?

I'm sorry about your foot

CYNTHIA. Don't be sorry

GABRIEL. Congratulations then

CYNTHIA. Thank you

> *He is still hugging her. It's long, silent and awkward.*

CYNTHIA. Don't get attracted to me

GABRIEL. Ha ha

CYNTHIA. Sorry. I regret that. I regret that joke
   Okay
   I'm going to let go now

GABRIEL. You don't have to

CYNTHIA. No. I'm going to let go. In 5 seconds.

   Ten seconds. She lets go.

CYNTHIA. Whew. That was intense, man. That was hard. I thought maybe I'd never let go. I thought maybe we'd be stuck together like those people they shame?

GABRIEL. I don't know

CYNTHIA. Those people they shame by tying them together?

GABRIEL. You feel better?

CYNTHIA. Thank you

GABRIEL. You're welcome

CYNTHIA. *(making to exit)* I think I'm gonna go rejoin the troops

GABRIEL. Cynthia?

CYNTHIA. Yes

GABRIEL. I hear you put a ring on your finger

CYNTHIA. Oh, um. Yup

GABRIEL. Who's the lucky guy?

CYNTHIA. Arthur

GABRIEL. Arthur. That's great. That's really– I'm happy for you.

CYNTHIA. Thanks. I should go check on Carol. See if she needs help

GABRIEL. What does Arthur do?

CYNTHIA. Oh. Um. He has his own brand of vitamins. You drink them. They don't taste too bad. Kinda earthy.

GABRIEL. Well sounds like he'll be a good provider

CYNTHIA. He is.

GABRIEL. That's great. That's just great.

CYNTHIA. Okay

GABRIEL. Okay

CYNTHIA. Nice brushing with you

GABRIEL. Is there– Is there– Is there a wedding?

CYNTHIA. There is.

GABRIEL. That's great.

CYNTHIA. It's just, um, close friends. It's just, you know, intimates.

GABRIEL. I'll have to get you a lemon zester

CYNTHIA. We really don't need anything

GABRIEL. Or whatever you want

CYNTHIA. It's just, uh, people who know both of us. Who are, you know, part of our lives. It's a tiny ceremony, really. 16, 18 people–

GABRIEL. He should just kidnap you–

CYNTHIA. My limit is 25–

GABRIEL. He should just surprise you one day and grab you and haul you off and kidnap you and you can just skip the whole thing

CYNTHIA. Ha ha

GABRIEL. That's what I would do. If I could do it again.

> *Cynthia smiles.*

GABRIEL. It'd be nice to get close again.

CYNTHIA. Yeah

GABRIEL. It'd be nice to have you as part of our lives again.

CYNTHIA. Here I am.

GABRIEL. I'm so happy to see you

> *She smiles. Gabriel reaches out his hands and tickles her very lightly on her ribs.*

GABRIEL. Tick-tick-tick

CYNTHIA. Haha stop

GABRIEL. Tick-tick-tick

CYNTHIA. Stop it

GABRIEL. Tick-tick-tick-tick

CYNTHIA. Gabriel! I'm serious. Knock it off.

GABRIEL. But you're laughing you're laughing

CYNTHIA. I'm not

> *Gabriel stops.*

CYNTHIA. I'm going to go ask Carol where to shit.

———————

> *Carol is packing a suitcase in the master bedroom.*
> *She pulls a tan blouse out of shopping bag. Gabriel*
> *enters.*

GABRIEL. Almost done?

CAROL. What's this?

GABRIEL. Oh, that's a present. It's– You're not supposed to see that. I was going to give it to you on Mother's Day.

CAROL. Is it for a nurse?

GABRIEL. Huh?

CAROL. What is it? Is it something a nurse would wear?

GABRIEL. Huh?

CAROL. A smock? A smock for a nurse?

GABRIEL. Put it on

CAROL. In a minute.

> *Carol flops on the bed.*

CAROL. ARRRRG

GABRIEL. Take a break

CAROL. Still wind

GABRIEL. Still wind

CAROL. Why? Why? Why does it wind?

GABRIEL. We should head out as soon as it lets up

CAROL. Sure, sure

GABRIEL. Find a hotel, er, some place with hot water... Uh, whoa. Are you masturbating?

CAROL. Hm?

GABRIEL. Why are you masturbating right now?

CAROL. These shorts have been driving me nuts all day

GABRIEL. Whoa, honey

CAROL. Why are you being so weird about this?

GABRIEL. It's just so…it's just so…whoa. Raw and real

CAROL. You've seen it before

GABRIEL. I know, but I– I just can't believe I get to see this, like, right now.

CAROL. You're a lucky guy

GABRIEL. I am very lucky

CAROL. I want you to tell me how horrible I am

GABRIEL. Why?

CAROL. Just do it

GABRIEL. No. Why?

CAROL. Why not?

GABRIEL. Are you sure?

CAROL. Just do it. I'm gonna be done in a second

GABRIEL. Okay. Um. Okay. Wow. This is tough. This is really tough. *(He clears his throat.)*
Okay, you are– Let me start over. You are– *(He clears his throat.)* Okay I'm a little nervous about this. You are totally incompetent. You are totally incompetent, um. You've been packing all day, and you're still not done. You are a slow packer. Um. You forget to do things. You, uh, you don't do the dishes. You don't do the laundry. You don't do the laundry sometimes. You think whatever is stressing you out in your life is more important than any of the people around you. You are a stress magnet. Um. You call me stupid. A lot. And you hit me. You really can't hit me, Carol, even though you're physically small, you shouldn't hit me. And you yell too much. You don't know how to talk to Kayden sometimes. If I try to have sex with you and you don't want to, you're mean to me sometimes. You… Uh, Carol?

CAROL. Yeah?

GABRIEL. Should I– Should I keep going?

CAROL. No, I think you should stop

GABRIEL. Did you like that?

CAROL. No

>   *Long pause.*

CAROL. I just wanted you to tell me that I'm a bad girl

GABRIEL. What?

CAROL. All I wanted was for you to tell me that I'm a bad, bad girl

GABRIEL. Oh. I'm sorry.

CAROL. It's okay

GABRIEL. Do you want me to go down on you?

CAROL. No

GABRIEL. Can I kiss you?

>   *Silence.*

CAROL. When I hit you, it's a joke

GABRIEL. What?

CAROL. It's just joking, when I hit you

GABRIEL. I know

CAROL. I thought you liked it

GABRIEL. I do. I do like it

>   *Carol gets up, grabs the blouse and exits into the*
>   *bathroom.*

GABRIEL. Where are you going?

CAROL. I'm going to go try this on in front of the mirror

>   *Gabriel picks up some clothes and puts them in the*
>   *suitcase. Carol enters in the tan smock, weeping.*

GABRIEL. Let me see

CAROL. What do you think?

GABRIEL. I'll give it to Cynthia, if you don't like it

CAROL. Don't give it to Cynthia. I'll find some use for it. I'll wear it under something. I need a neutral top for some of my skirts, I–

It doesn't fit my body right

GABRIEL. Huh?

CAROL. Do you think it fits my body right?

GABRIEL. Uh, yeah, I think it fits pretty good–

CAROL. Why would you get me something so bland?

———————

Kayden and Barbara's bedroom. Kayden and Cynthia sit up in twin beds. They both wear winter jackets with hoods. Barbara tucks Kayden in very tight. It's a little scary.

CYNTHIA. Do you remember that stand-up swimming pool that that mom, that *other* mom
That friend of Carol's who was also a mom

BARBARA. Ashley!

CYNTHIA. No, with the foster kids

BARBARA. Oh, Melissa

CYNTHIA. Who was always squeezing your–

BARBARA. Who was always squeezing your shoulders!

CYNTHIA. And she brought over that stand-up swimming pool so that Carol could teach me how to swim?

BARBARA. (How are you doing, Kayden? Can you move?)

KAYDEN. (No)

BARBARA. (Good)

Barbara puts a sleep mask shaped like a butterfly over Kayden's eyes.

BARBARA. *(to Cynthia)* She gets scared when she can see things in the dark

CYNTHIA. And you were teaching me to open my eyes under the water
And we were sitting at the bottom of the pool on the you know plastic

And the water pushed the straps of your swimsuit off
your shoulders

And I saw that your breasts were attached to your
swimsuit

That you didn't have any breasts

That you just had your scars

BARBARA. (Are your eyes closed, Kayden?)

KAYDEN. (No)

BARBARA. (Honey close your eyes)

CYNTHIA. And I shot up with my arms up

Straight up, like I was diving up into the air

And Carol grabbed me by the arm

And lifted me out of the pool by the arm

And dragged me over to the sunlight with my arms up

And she stared at my armpit really hard

And then she said in front of everyone– Melissa and her
foster kids and you and Gabriel

Like she was angry

You. You. You need to start shaving

BARBARA. I don't remember that

I remember Melissa and the stand-up pool but I don't
remember that

KAYDEN. (Am I breathing?)

BARBARA. (What honey?)

KAYDEN. (Am I breathing?)

BARBARA. (Yes, yes honey. Can't you feel it?)

CYNTHIA. And I spent the rest of the week

With those *hairs* under my arms

Waiting for someone to give me a razor

BARBARA. You want me to tuck you in?

CYNTHIA. You'd never tuck me in

BARBARA. Get under the covers I'll tuck you in

> *Cynthia gets under the covers. Carol appears in the
> doorway. Her face is covered in a dirty dishrag.*

BARBARA. I used to pick at Carol's acne. *(Barbara laughs.)* So bad. Bad, Barbara, bad! And I knew it was bad. I told her it'd make it better, but I knew it was bad. I couldn't help myself. I just liked doing it.

CYNTHIA. It's cold. Don't you think it's cold?

BARBARA. Here have some gum

> *Barbara rips a piece of paper and puts it in Cynthia's mouth. She chews.*

BARBARA. Kayden? You want some gum?

> *Kayden opens her mouth. Barbara pops in a piece of paper. Then she rips a piece for herself.*

BARBARA. Now we all have some gum and we can go to sleep

> *They try to sleep.*

BARBARA. You'll have to tell me about Arthur.

CYNTHIA. *(seeing Carol)* Oh god

BARBARA. Not right now. I'm tired. But sometime before you leave we'll sit down and you can tell me about Arthur.

> *Carol approaches Cynthia with the dishrag on her face. Maybe she makes a low, guttural noise under the dishrag.*

CYNTHIA. Oh god

BARBARA. *(seeing Carol)* Ope, she's gonna get you!
She's gonna get you, Cynthia!
She's gonna get you!

> *Carol looms over Cynthia, the dishrag still on her face. She lifts her hands slowly to the corners of the dishrag…*

CYNTHIA. Carol, I'm not joking
I'm looking you straight in the eye and I'm saying no
I'm saying no
I'm saying no, Carol
I'm an adult and I'm saying no

Carol lunges at Cynthia, covering Cynthia's face with the dishrag.

It gets dark. Really, really dark. Maybe we can't see anything.

Kayden jumps on the trampoline. A small figure going up and down in the dark. There is thunder in the distance. Maybe some of her jumps are illuminated by lightning. She goes from glee to terror and back again. A huge crack of thunder and she's gone.

The moon comes out. Barbara and Kayden asleep in one bed. Carol and Cynthia are entwined in the other – limbs tangled. Maybe Carol's head is in Cynthia's lap. Cynthia plays with Carol's hair.

CYNTHIA. Picture yourself dead. Like really dead. Like ugly dead. Like someone slit your throat, okay? And there's blood everywhere. All over your face. Just dead dead, okay? And we're all at your funeral. And you can't even fit in your casket because your legs are broken, okay? Someone broke your legs. You're just kinda sitting up in your coffin – dead – like crippled like twisted in there like propped up in your coffin and everyone is pointing at you and they're saying: "She was awful." "Oh god, she was awful." "Awful awful."

CAROL. Okay

CYNTHIA. Just make yourself feel as bad as possible

Carol does.

CYNTHIA. And then draw a line right here. And release it. All those bad thoughts just–

Cynthia draws a line with her fingernail from her wrist to the underside of her elbow, very slowly.

CYNTHIA. There. See.

Do you want one?

Carol wants one but she's a little afraid to do it.

CYNTHIA. Trust me. It makes you feel better. You just take all of the pain and frustration you're feeling. And you put it into that line. It's like cutting yourself but you just draw a line right here.

CAROL. I don't cut myself

CYNTHIA. I know but if you get that sort of impulse

CAROL. I don't have impulses like that

CYNTHIA. Sure you do. Everybody does

Cynthia takes Carol's wrist.

CYNTHIA. Just one.

Cynthia draws a line with her fingernail from Carol's armpit to her wrist very slowly. It feels really good. Carol is in ecstasy.

CYNTHIA. There see

The bedroom window blows out. Huge crash.

CAROL. Oh my–

BARBARA. We're okay! Are we okay?

CAROL. Are you okay? I think I'm okay. I seem okay

CYNTHIA. I'm okay

They start to laugh.

BARBARA. Where is Kayden
I've lost Kayden

CYNTHIA. Where is Kayden

CAROL. Kayden where are you?

BARBARA. It's her feet! It's her feet!
She's got her head at the bottom of the bed
And it's just her feet!

———————

Everyone has invaded Carol and Gabriel's bedroom. They all wear glow sticks around their necks and wrists. Gabriel wears one like a headband and it looks like a halo.

> *Maybe they all sit on the bed. Maybe they've*
> *dragged the trampoline into the bedroom and sit*
> *on it instead.*

CAROL. *(with newfound energy, even happiness)* It's like never
being alone
It's like having someone who's always on your side
Who knows your secrets and still loves you
And sees you as you really are: complex and deep and
full of life and just *radiant*

GABRIEL. It's like having the most generous, patient and
wise lover you've ever imagined in your heart with you
always

CYNTHIA. I'm not sure I'd like that

CAROL. Just ask

CYNTHIA. Jesus come into my heart?

CAROL. Yes, just like that

CYNTHIA. *Jesus come into my heart*

CAROL. He's there

CYNTHIA. Really?

CAROL. Yup, all you had to do is ask

CYNTHIA. He's there right now?

CAROL. Yup, He's there. He's right in there

BARBARA. Should we pray?

CAROL. Yes! Let's pray

> *Carol, Barbara, Gabriel and Kayden pray a well-*
> *known prayer with simple hand gestures.*

CAROL, BARBARA, GABRIEL, KAYDEN. Lord be in mine head,
and in mine understanding
Lord be in mine eyes, and in mine looking
Lord be in mine lips, and in mine speaking
Lord be in mine heart, and in mine thinking
Lord be at mine end, and at mine departing
Amen

> *They sit in silence.*

GABRIEL. Life is so exciting!

CAROL. You think?

GABRIEL. Yeah! This is exciting! The lights are out. There's glow sticks. The wind can get inside the house. Don't you feel a little happy?

CAROL. A little

Cynthia picks up a big white candle.

CYNTHIA. This is the Jesus candle

CAROL. What?

CYNTHIA. I'm going to light this candle and Jesus will be in the room

CAROL. Oh, I don't know if I like that

CYNTHIA. Dear Jesus, please come into this candle

CAROL. You're making fun of me

CYNTHIA. I'm not. I mean it. Jesus please come into this candle.

She lights the candle.

CYNTHIA. See. He's here. He's here with us.

GABRIEL. That's nice. That's a nice gesture, Cynthia. I appreciate that.

BARBARA. Does anyone want more tuna?

KAYDEN. I do

BARBARA. Somebody's gotta finish this tuna. We've just got a couple of / spoonfuls left.

CAROL. Cynthia. Is there anything you want to pray about in particular?

CYNTHIA. Oh. Um. Not really.

CAROL. It can be anything at all. Anything you want to get off your chest

CYNTHIA. Out loud?

GABRIEL. Not if you don't / want

CAROL. She should do it out loud

CYNTHIA. I can do it out loud. I'm not, um, shy.

CAROL. Don't even think of it as praying. Don't even– Just forget Jesus for a second. Just put Jesus over there on that shelf. We'll get him later. And just shut your eyes for a minute. Close your eyes. And just go deep down. Deep down to your deepest darkest thoughts. To your deepest darkest self and–

CYNTHIA. Talk?

CAROL. That's how I do it.

CYNTHIA. Okay. Um. I am–

CAROL. And just say whatever you want. Whatever feels true to you.

CYNTHIA. Okay. I am sad?

CAROL. Good

GABRIEL. Good

CYNTHIA. I don't like myself very much?

CAROL. It doesn't have to be negative. It can be anything

CYNTHIA. I guess I'm just feeling kinda negative right now

CAROL. That's okay too

CYNTHIA. Um

CAROL. Close your eyes. What do you see?

CYNTHIA. Black.

CAROL. Good and– Okay. Why don't we all do this together? As a group? Let's just pray for things we need. Things we need and/or want. / Okay. I'll start. I pray for good weather

GABRIEL. I pray for the safety of all those in our community. And our city. And our state. And our president. The whole world, Jesus. Keep us all– Keep everybody safe.

CAROL. Patience

GABRIEL. For JD Burr's cancer and for his wife Mandy

CAROL. Um. Love. I pray for self-love. For everybody

BARBARA. We pray for the repose of the souls of those who have departed. For my mother, Hazel. For my father, Harold. For my sister, Elda. May they bask in the glow of your eternal kingdom, Lord Jesus

CAROL. Calmness.

GABRIEL. For Wilson.

Silence.

CYNTHIA. I pray that I get home to Arthur. And that we have a beautiful wedding. And start a beautiful family together.

CAROL. Good, Cynthia. That's so good!

GABRIEL. That's really nice, Cynthia. That's a nice prayer.

KAYDEN. I pray for the people who don't have any families

CAROL. That's good too, Kayden

GABRIEL. That is also a very good prayer

CAROL. Now is there anything you want Jesus to forgive you for? Anything you want to get off your chest.

CYNTHIA. Um. Jesus. Sometimes I think I try too hard?

CAROL. Uh-huh. Anything else?

CYNTHIA. Um.

GABRIEL. Actually I have something I would like to– May I? *(he clears his throat)* I just– I just want to take a moment to humble myself before you, Jesus. And to humble myself before everyone. Because there is someone in this room who I have taken for granted.

Carol looks at Gabriel, touched.

GABRIEL. There is someone in this room who I have somehow failed to fully appreciate the...gorgeous, alive being that she is. And I love her so much. And I want to spend the rest of my life making it up to her. (Cynthia? Sweetheart? Can you open your eyes? I want to say this to you directly. Thank you.) Cynthia? Do you forgive me?

CYNTHIA. Oh, um. Yes. I mean, yes! I do.

Cynthia and Gabriel hug.

BARBARA. Lord, I truly forgive my mother.
I forgive her for all the times she hurt me, she resented me, she was angry with me and for all the times she punished me. I forgive her for the times she preferred

my sister to me. I forgive her for the times she told me I was dumb, ugly, stupid, the worst of the children or that I cost the family a lot of money. For the times she told me I was unwanted, an accident, a mistake or not what she expected, I forgive her.

 Silence.

CAROL. Okay. Well. Blessings. Does anyone have any blessings? Anything they're thankful for?

CYNTHIA. Gabriel

CAROL. Okay. Um. I am thankful for Barbara

BARBARA. Oh!

KAYDEN. Imagination

 Late that night. The Jesus Candle has burnt down low. Gabriel and Cynthia are hunched over it, praying. They are really, really into it – almost out of control. Gabriel has one hand on Cynthia's head like a blessing. They are sweating. Kayden is asleep. Carol and Barbara lurk in the shadows. Their glow sticks are very dim.

CYNTHIA. I might be freaking out more than I should be. I just need God right now more than ever! I am going through some tough times. I am just so full of rage and sickness and despair about everything everything. I cry all the time. I cry every day. **GABRIEL**. Help her I just keep talking shit about   Lord Jesus. Hear her people even though I want   Lord Jesus to stop talking shit about people. I tell myself I'm going

to stop talking shit about people
and then I just keep doing it. I keep
talking shit. Please help me to stop.
I'm just filled with rage. I don't
know why. Like every day every day
ARRRRG like I'm walking down
the street and I just want to rip out
people's assholes because of the way
they walk, or how slow they walk,
or because they keep commenting
on everything, commenting on the
sun and the weather and the flowers
and the dresses in the window and
I just want them to shut the fuck
up because they're ruining it for
me by talking about it. Because
it's all ugly when they say it. And I
know it's lame to feel that way but
I can't help it because I'm full of
rage. All the time. For as long as
I can remember. I'm just full of
rage. Because *everything everything*
is lies and *everything everything* is
exhausting and every tiny good
thing you build for yourself takes so
much work and so much sacrifice
and nobody else even cares and the
amount of sadness in the world and
the amount of stupid stupid dumb
dumb obligation and everything
is lies but you don't realize it until
you're a grown up and it's too late
to change anything because the lies
have grown into you and grown into
your skin and you can't be separated
from the lies like those people who
have a metal stake in their brains
and you can't take the metal stake
out or they'll die so they just have

Help her
Lord Jesus

It's okay to be
angry. It's okay
to express
your anger.
It's okay to let
it all out and
be mad

to live with a metal stake in their
brains for the rest of their life and
everybody's walking around like
that and you're just supposed to
keep going and keep pretending
And everyone thinks I'm a bitch
but actually I'm just really easily
intimidated and I don't know how
to talk to people and I'm actually
really shy and I don't hear things
that well like actually I think
I'm losing my hearing and so
sometimes I don't hear the things
that people say to me and so I just
don't know how to respond so I
just mouth words, I don't even
say them I just mouth them, like
"thank you" like on the street like
some guy asks me what time it is
and I just mouth the words "thank
you" because I don't know what's
going on and then he thinks I'm
a bitch because I don't tell him
the time but actually I'm just
intimidated and feeling vulnerable
and I feel vulnerable all the time. I
cry all the time. And Arthur called
me because he wanted to move
the wedding to the summer and
I thought he was maybe going
to cancel it but actually he just
wanted to do it in the summer and
I got so scared that he was leaving
me that I just started shitting in a
plastic bag I couldn't even make
it to the bathroom I just grabbed
a plastic bag from off the floor
and started shitting in it in my
bedroom while he was on the

Hear her
Lord Jesus

Do you feel
Him here with
you, honey?

phone and all he was saying was that we should get married in August and my body just started shitting because I was so scared that everything was ending and I would be all alone. I just need something to hold on to. I just need something to hold on to. Jesus Christ God please help me. Please just be with me

GABRIEL. He's here, He's here, Cynthia. You are doing so great. I am so proud of you. You are really just soaring. / Just soaring to another plane of– Yes, yes. Just let it go. Just ride it. Let it take you. Whatever you need to get off your chest. Just give it to Jesus and He will take it from you

CYNTHIA. Also I read a lot of erotic fiction. Like really trashy ones. Like before they got politically correct. And I think I should stop. Please help me to stop. Like my favorite one – don't kill me for this – but my favorite one is about this Sultan who like abducts this lady or whatever and there's one moment where he just yanks her over her knee and spanks her like not a real spanking just like 3 really good swats and. Oh man. That made me– Like, I couldn't stand it. It was. Really. Intense. I shouldn't read that shit anymore, right? I'm going to stop reading that shit. I know I should've stopped reading that shit. That's it. I'm cut off. No more. *Jesus.* I think I need some water. We might need to take a break here. I'm sweating. I think I need a bottle of water. Who's there? Did they all go to sleep?

CAROL. We're still here

CYNTHIA. What time is it?

CAROL. We should start thinking about bed

CYNTHIA. Do we have any more water?

CAROL. I'll get you some

> *Carol exits.*

CYNTHIA. Jesus. How long have I been talking? I hope I haven't– I hope I haven't been hogging the floor or– Anyone else have something they wanted to say?

Silence.

GABRIEL. Last night I dreamed that Carol was eaten by lions

CYNTHIA. Was it gory?

GABRIEL. No, I don't think so. She's just "Not Eaten." And then she's "Eaten." And there are lions present.

Barbara is laughing.

GABRIEL. What?

BARBARA. Nothing, nothing. I'm thinking about something that happened to my sister and I can't remember if it happened or she dreamed it. Isn't that funny?

CYNTHIA. That happens to me all the time

GABRIEL. What is it?

BARBARA. No, no I can't

CYNTHIA. Come on

BARBARA. Oh, Lordy. I think I have to tell it. *(sighs)* Oh, my. It's just. There was this pickle and she was being–

CYNTHIA. This is a dream

BARBARA. No, no, I think this really happened. There was this pickle and she was being– This man was– The pickle was *there.*

CYNTHIA. Where?

BARBARA. You know where. And then the man bit off the end of the pickle. So there wasn't a nub. It was just bit off

They are all laughing

CYNTHIA. Oh Jesus oh Jesus

BARBARA. Stuck up in there

GABRIEL. This happened to Elda, you're saying this happened to Elda?

BARBARA. I think it happened to Elda. I think it really happened. Oh, she would kill me. / She would just kill me. It's funny isn't it? I mean, she thought it was funny, but she would kill me. Now how am I supposed to eat a pickle? How am I supposed to eat a whole pickle in my life again? Tell me! How am I supposed to eat a pickle?

CYNTHIA. Oh, man. I love this. I love this story.

GABRIEL. I have the same thing with tuna fish and applesauce. I ate one then the other and then vomited and now applesauce always reminds me of vomit / and tuna fish I can't even bear the thought of eating it

BARBARA. And this one here, Cynthia, she used to suck on pickles. Keep them in her cheek like a little chipmunk. / It used to turn my stomach just looking at you. Sucking on that pickle. Now tell me, how am I supposed to eat a pickle again?

CYNTHIA. Oh I really love you guys. I really, really love you guys.

They laugh. Carol enters with water.

CAROL. I'm sorry I missed the party.

CYNTHIA. Sorry, Carol. I should've gotten my own water.

CAROL. Where's Kayden?

BARBARA. She's asleep here somewhere

CYNTHIA. Where'd she go?

GABRIEL. Kayden

BARBARA. We keep losing Kayden!

CAROL. Shhh Don't wake her!

They feel around in the dark

BARBARA. *(from across the room, maybe under the trampoline)* Here she is. Over here. She's sleeping. Here she is.

CAROL. Shh

BARBARA. Oh it's so wonderful to feel her sleeping here in the dark. She's very warm.

Barbara carries Kayden into the bathroom. Carol lingers in the doorway.

CAROL. Cynthia? You wanna come brush your teeth?

CYNTHIA. In a minute

CAROL. Should I keep a light lit for you?

GABRIEL. You go ahead, Carol. I'll get her a light.

Carol exits to the bathroom.

CYNTHIA. Oh man

GABRIEL. We should go to bed

CYNTHIA. What about the candle?

GABRIEL. Blow it out

CYNTHIA. No!

GABRIEL. We have to

CYNTHIA. We can't just blow the Jesus Candle out!

GABRIEL. Don't be silly, it's just a candle

CYNTHIA. Let's just sleep here. Let's just lie down and sleep here on the floor until it burns out.

GABRIEL. Cynthia. I'm going to blow the candle out. And when I blow the candle out the light of the world that is Jesus is going to turn into smoke. And that smoke is going to fill the air. And we will breathe that air into our lungs and he will be part of us. Okay?

Gabriel blows out the candle. Gabriel and Cynthia in the dark sniffing the smoke.

———————

A huge crash. The attic caves in. The storm is closer now and more violent. Sections of the house are falling off and flying away. Debris from the outside world is flying in – umbrellas, patio furniture, papers, creatures, and things from far away. Kayden and Barbara's bedroom is wrecked. Carol and Gabriel's bedroom is wrecked. Carol and Cynthia use all the furniture in the house to build a barricade and keep the storm out.

Kayden and Barbara have taken refuge in the bathroom. The bathtub has been turned into a little bed for Kayden.

A giant crab appears on the rim of the bathtub.

BARBARA. Kayden?

KAYDEN. Yes?

BARBARA. Where did you get that crab?

KAYDEN. The living room

BARBARA. Is it dead?

KAYDEN. I don't know. Where's my dad?

BARBARA. He's outside fixing the siding. Come here. Sit on my lap.

> *Kayden crawls into Barbara's lap, still holding the crab.*

BARBARA. Are you scared of the storm?

(Kayden doesn't answer.)

BARBARA. Listen. What do you hear? Do you hear that howling? What's that?

KAYDEN. Wind

BARBARA. That's right. It's only wind. Wind can't hurt us, can it? And what's that crack?

KAYDEN. Tree

BARBARA. We would've cut those trees down anyway in five to ten years.

KAYDEN. Hooves!

BARBARA. No. That's glass. And thunder

KAYDEN. Someone crying

BARBARA. That's a dog

KAYDEN. Oh. My dad?

BARBARA. It's not your dad. It's a dog.

> *Gabriel enters with a bloody hand.*

GABRIEL. I tripped.

> *He wraps his hand in toilet paper and then heads back out into the storm.*

———————

Gabriel stands with his back against the door to the bathroom. A final stand. He holds a hammer and nails. His hand is bandaged and bloody. The storm is inside the house. He talks to it.

GABRIEL. So what's the plan?

Are you gonna stop, or should I just go for it?

I'd like it if you'd stop.

That's what I'd prefer, if you're curious.

I'm just gonna do this real quick and go back inside there. 5 minutes tops.

I won't even look at you, I promise.

The wind dies down.

GABRIEL. There. See. That wasn't so hard was it?

I appreciate that, really I– Thank you.

Okay I'm just going to do this real quick.

He hammers a plank across the doorway to the master bedroom.

A little gust of wind.

GABRIEL. Don't do it!

Another little gust of wind.

GABRIEL. Come on, baby. I know you don't wanna do this. Easy, easy. Just keep it easy. That's right. That's right, my darling. We're doing this! We're doing it. We're doing so good! I love you right now. We're doing it–

A gust of wind. A piece of debris flies up and hits Gabriel hard in the face.

GABRIEL. God Dammit!

He catches himself.

GABRIEL. It's okay. It's okay.

I'm not angry.

I was cocky. I was arrogant. I overreached.

Another piece of debris hits him in the face.

GABRIEL. Ow. That really hurt.

Ouch, ow. That hurt really bad. *Really bad.* Ow.

He is on the verge of tears.

GABRIEL. I'm just gonna take it slow.

Do whatever you want.

Do whatever you need.

I won't stop you. Just pretend I'm not here... Pretend you can't even see me.

I'm just gonna...

He hammers tentatively.

GABRIEL. That's all. Nice and slow and–

He hammers tentatively.

GABRIEL. We've got this.

You've got this, Gabriel, you've got this.

Come on, baby, you've got this.

Don't be afraid, baby. You've got this.

I love you baby, you've got this.

I'm proud of you, baby, you've got this.

You've got this, sweetheart, you've got this.

> *As Gabriel hammers, the wind dies. The rain stops. The sounds of the storm slowly fades into the sounds of early, early dawn – birds, insects. It crescendos into a cacophony of restless creatures.*
>
> *Kayden screams. It's morning and the light is bright. Everybody is crammed in the bathroom. Kayden has a bloody nose. There is blood all over her face.*

CYNTHIA. Oh my god! Sorry! It was a total accident!

GABRIEL. What's going on?

Kayden is sobbing inconsolably.

CYNTHIA. I hit her in the face. I was sleeping and when I woke up I just hit her in the face. I'm sorry, Kayden, I'm sorry. I just woke up and I hit her in the face

GABRIEL. Ay yi yi Oh honey

CAROL. Give her to me. Tilt your head back honey

KAYDEN. Thuhsblaaaeeeenmaaaaamoooow *[i.e., There is blood in my mouth]*

CYNTHIA. I just woke up and I hit her in the face. My arm just– My arm just went

CAROL. It'll stop in a second, honey, we just gotta let the blood clot form

KAYDEN. Maaaaaaathuhsblaaaeeeenmaaaaamoooow *[i.e., Mom, there's blood in my mouth]*

CYNTHIA. I don't know what happened. I woke up and my arm just went straight into her nose

CAROL. Tilt your head back honey

KAYDEN. THERE IS BLOOD IN MY MOUTH! THERE IS BLOOD IN MY MOUTH!

> *Kayden coughs up blood onto the carpet.*

CAROL. Oh sorry, baby. I'm so, so sorry

BARBARA. Carol, listen–

> *Silence – no storm.*

———————————

> *Everyone is crammed into the bloody car with the deer-sized hole in the windshield. Carol holds the dead Jedediah – wrapped in a sheet – in her lap. Kayden holds a tissue to her nose. She is curled up against Carol. After a minute…*

GABRIEL. Oh. The radio. I completely forgot we had the radio.

Gabriel switches on the radio. The warm, smooth sound of Beyoncé comes pouring out.* Cynthia sings along. Carol joins her. Cynthia stretches her arms out the window. It is divine.

The following dialogue eventually starts under the music...

BARBARA. I need to use the ladies room

KAYDEN. Dad what's a clot?

GABRIEL. Sorry Mom are you talking to me?

BARBARA. I need to use the ladies room whenever you get a chance to pullover

KAYDEN. Dad what's a clot?

CAROL. So what's the plan Gabriel?

GABRIEL. I'm sorry, I'm going deaf

BARBARA. The ladies room!   CAROL. I said what's the plan

GABRIEL. The plan is drive to a town with power and find a hotel

CYNTHIA. How far do you think we'll have to go?

GABRIEL. I don't know. Maybe Omak?

KAYDEN. Mom

CYNTHIA. Oh my god, seriously, Omak?

KAYDEN. Mom

CYNTHIA. Oh my god, I'm already nauseous

CAROL. What baby?

KAYDEN. What's a clot?

CAROL. It's something that stops you from bleeding to death, okay? Don't worry about it.

CYNTHIA. How far is Omak, Dad?

GABRIEL. 2 hours, 3 hours, 2 hours?

CAROL. Do you think the hotels will be full, Gabriel?

GABRIEL. I think you can answer that question just as well as I can, Carol

---

*Please see Music Use Note on page 3

BARBARA. I really do need to use the ladies room, I'm not trying to be difficult

CYNTHIA. Well, if we're going 3 hours…

GABRIEL. What's that, sweetheart?

CYNTHIA. I said, if we're going 3 hours, you guys might as well come to my place

> *Silence.*

GABRIEL. Well, that's very generous of you, sweetheart

CAROL. We wouldn't want to invade your private space

CYNTHIA. No, no you're not invading

CAROL. But do you have room?

BARBARA. Don't worry about me, if it's me you're worried about. I can sleep anywhere.

GABRIEL. How far is it? 5 hours?

CYNTHIA. Five, five and a half

GABRIEL. Hm

CAROL. I wouldn't want to put you out

CYNTHIA. You could meet Arthur

GABRIEL. I don't know, Carol, sounds kinda fun

CAROL. You two decide, then. Whatever you want

GABRIEL. Well, I'll tell you one thing. I am not going five and a half hours with that thing in the car

CAROL. Well then you can drop me off on the side of the road because I'm not–

BARBARA. Hey now

GABRIEL. Now seriously, Carol, come on. He's starting to smell. I don't know why you–

> *Carol clutches Jedediah.*

GABRIEL. You think he'd care? You think he'd care if we dropped him off by the side of the road? I think he'd be honored.

CAROL. I care

GABRIEL. I think it'd be a great testament to Jedediah if we left him in some field for other animals to come and sniff and roll in.I think he'd like that, personally. I think that's a very nice tribute

CYNTHIA. I'd say you could bury him at my place, but I don't have a yard

CAROL. I just–

GABRIEL. Don't get emotional

CAROL. I want to know where he is. I want to be able to visit the spot.

CYNTHIA. *(seeing something out the window)* Look

BARBARA. Look

CAROL. Oh my god, Gabriel, look

> *Gabriel stops the car. They look in silence for a minute.*

CAROL. Roll down the window

BARBARA. Don't stare

GABRIEL. Maybe electrical

CYNTHIA. All burnt up

> *Long time staring.*

> *Gabriel starts up the car again and drives slowly.*

BARBARA. It just keeps going, doesn't it?

CAROL. (Careful, Gabriel)

GABRIEL. (I'll go around it)

BARBARA. I would've thought we would've driven out of it by now but it just keeps going…

CAROL. I feel so bad about the birds

> *They drive in silence – just the radio. Gabriel switches the radio off.*

BARBARA. Gabriel? Do you see that nice clump of trees over there? Why don't you pull off there and I'll just go run to the restroom real quick.

———————

A field by the edge of the woods.

Cynthia and Gabriel dig a shallow grave for Jedediah at the foot of a tree using an ice-scraper as a shovel. Cynthia does the digging.

CYNTHIA. Is that deep enough?

GABRIEL. I think it's about as deep as it's gonna get

CYNTHIA. She's gonna want it deeper

GABRIEL. Well. Then she can dig the hole

CYNTHIA. Oof. Creepy!

GABRIEL. It's just a grave.

CYNTHIA. I mean, the woods. Doesn't it feel wrong to be here?

GABRIEL. What's gonna get you? There are no bears, / bobcats

CYNTHIA. Psychopaths. I'm more afraid of psycopaths

GABRIEL. People don't do that kind of thing during natural disasters

CYNTHIA. They don't?

GABRIEL. Why are you afraid of psychopaths?

CYNTHIA. I'm gonna dig it deeper

> *Cynthia digs.*

> *Barbara, Kayden and Carol emerge from the car. They are wobbly-legged, clutching their coats and a thermos. They stop to pee somewhere in the middle of the field. They can see Gabriel and Cynthia in the distance.*

CAROL. It feels balmy out here, don't you think it feels balmy

BARBARA. It reminds me of Guatemala

CAROL. Mmmm I love it

KAYDEN. I don't have to go to the bathroom

CAROL. Yes you do

KAYDEN. I do not

CAROL. Or you will

KAYDEN. Mom

BARBARA. Well I for one am going to go to the bathroom

CAROL. Me too

> *Barbara and Carol take off coats, undo-belts, etc. and squat to pee.*

> *Cynthia digging.*

CAROL. They're digging

BARBARA. Where?

CAROL. Over by that tree

> *Barbara waves.*

BARBARA. HELLO

CYNTHIA. HELLO

BARBARA. YOU FOUND A GOOD SPOT?

CYNTHIA. WHAT?

BARBARA. IS THE GROUND SOFT?

CYNTHIA. WE'RE ALMOST DONE

BARBARA. WE'RE JUST GOING TO THE BATHROOM

CYNTHIA. They're going to the bathroom.
Shoot. I should've done that.

GABRIEL. Smell that

CYNTHIA. What?

GABRIEL. The trees. What exactly is going on inside your nose that makes it smells that *good*?

CYNTHIA. Little pieces of the pine needle

> *He breathes it in.*

GABRIEL. Oh yeah. I feel high

> *Cynthia takes a big breath in.*

GABRIEL. I feel like I'm really far away. Like I'm on another planet.

CYNTHIA. It's dark in here. You could really sneak up on someone

GABRIEL. Uh, yeah. Ha. Yeah. You could.

Carol pees in the field.

CAROL. See Kayden, you wanna squat with your bottom facing uphill, so that the pee runs away from you. Sometimes you can even sit on a little log or rock and use it like a toilet. I know it looks like you're going to pee on your pants, but you're not, the angle of the, uh, the angle of the stream, there's some projectile motion going on, so I know it looks like you're going to pee on your pants but actually it goes right past your pants, I promise, as long as your pants are at your ankles, it goes right past your pants. It's no big deal. See. We're peeing. This is fun

BARBARA. Isn't it fun, Kayden? It's very fun

CAROL. Then you use a little leaf or stick or something to wipe yourself

BARBARA. But be careful. Not any leaf

CAROL. No not any leaf. Maybe a little stick is safer

BARBARA. Yeah, tell her to use a little stick.

CAROL. You're not going to do it, are you? She's not going to do it, see what did I tell you. Why are you so precious with yourself, Kayden? It's no big deal. Seriously no one cares about seeing you naked.

CYNTHIA. I've gotta pee
Shoot, I've really gotta pee
I'm just going to go behind this tree and pee, is that okay?

GABRIEL. You did a good job on this hole, Cynthia. I'm impressed.

CAROL. *(to Kayden)* Well don't come crying to me later when you wet your pants.

      Cynthia pees behind a tree.

CYNTHIA. I can't believe I'm getting married.
I just wanna say that
I can't believe I'm getting married
Wow

I'm getting married
Wowr
That's my life, that's my biggest decision. I did it. Wow.
    I really did it.

GABRIEL. You did

CYNTHIA. It's dark

GABRIEL. The trees make it look darker than it is

CYNTHIA. But it feels dark
    And we're in the woods
    With the animals
    And they can smell us
    But we can't see them
    And they'll come and find us
    And we won't see them coming
    I'm so afraid to be here
    Isn't that sad?
    I think it's sad
    If I had to spend a night alone in the woods I would die
    That's so sad, Gabe, I think that's sad
    Gabe?
    Gabe?
    Where'd you go?
    Dad?
    I don't like this
    I really don't like this
    Oh god

BARBARA. Ope, he's gonna get her
    Look at that Kayden, he's gonna get her

>   *Gabe bolts out of the darkness and tackles her. She
>   screams.*

CYNTHIA. OH MY GOD OH MY GOD

>   *Gabe laughs*

I hate you I hate you

Gabe laughing

I hate you, I do, I really– I hate you

> *Carol appears holding the dead Jedediah, wrapped in sheet. Cynthia and Gabriel still lying on the forest floor.*

CAROL. You want me to bury you both together?

CYNTHIA. Do you like the hole, Carol?

CAROL. Is it deep enough?

CYNTHIA. Yeah, look, it's deep

GABRIEL. Where's Mom?

BARBARA. Here we are! We're walking through the trees

> *Barbara and Kayden approach, picking their way over roots and branches.*

BARBARA. Well, shall we?

I don't mean to be a spoilsport but it's getting late.

GABRIEL. Lay him in the grave, honey

> *Carol lays Jedediah in the grave.*

CAROL. I wish we had a coffin

GABRIEL. There. Perfect size, see.

CYNTHIA. Don't touch him, Kayden. Kayden? No touch.

GABRIEL. Kayden, want to put some dirt in?

> *Kayden drops two fistfuls of dirt into the grave.*

GABRIEL. There now. He's up in Heaven eating a big steak. Say goodbye, honey.

KAYDEN. Bye

> *Kayden reaches out to pet Jedediah*

GABRIEL. Don't touch him, honey. I'm gonna cover him up

CYNTHIA. Bye-bye, Kayden, say Bye-bye

CAROL. Hang on, I just–

BARBARA. Let her catch her breath

CAROL. I just wanted to say

BARBARA. Go on, dear

CAROL. Okay, um… Oh gosh

I loved you, Jedediah

I loved you so much

And I looked forward to seeing you every day

I looked forward to talking to you and telling you about my day

And lying with you on the floor. In the sunshine

I liked how you followed me around the house

And came into the bathroom

And leaned against my legs when you were being lazy and didn't want to stand up by yourself

And how you looked at me

You really knew me. I believe that

Cynthia sees something in the bushes.

You were a good friend

You really loved me

And I needed that

I needed you more than you'll ever know

And I loved you more than you'll ever know

And I wish there was some way for me to let you know how special you were to me

Because you meant the world to me, you really did.

And–

BARBARA. Are you okay?

CAROL. Yeah. Just one– And I loved you like a son.

BARBARA. Are you done?

CAROL. I guess. I guess I'm done.

CYNTHIA. Hey! Hey don't freak but there's something in the bushes

BARBARA. Where?

CYNTHIA. Over there. There's something in the bushes. I've heard it now. Three times. Fuck, fuck, fuck

They listen for a second – rustling.

CYNTHIA. There it is! There it is!

CAROL. It's coming! It's coming toward us

BARBARA. Gabriel! Get a stick!

GABRIEL. There are no sticks there are no sticks

CYNTHIA. Go for the eyes, then, just hit it in the eyes

GABRIEL. Stop. Everybody stop. Just freeze.

Everybody freezes. Long silence. Then Barbara runs straight toward the bushes.

BARBARA. GAAAAAHHHHH. GAHHHHHHHHHHH. GAAAAAAAAAAAAAAAAAHHHHHHHHH

The animal runs away.

CAROL. It's a dog! It's a dog! I saw its tail! It ran away!

CYNTHIA. It was just a dog. It was only a dog

CAROL. Oh no poor puppy. He's probably cold.

CYNTHIA. He's probably rabid, seriously, he's probably a dirty, dirty dog. Barbara's a hero

CAROL. Yes, Grandma the hero!!!

BARBARA. I'm not a hero

CYNTHIA. You are! You are! You saved us from the rabid dog!

CAROL. Maybe it was Jedediah. Maybe it was Jedediah's ghost

CYNTHIA. It was Jedediah's ghost!

CAROL. Oh my god it was! It was Jedediah's ghost

BARBARA. We should go

GABRIEL. We should really go

CYNTHIA. Oh my god it's ten o'clock we should go

CAROL. Hang on

Carol plants a stick upright on the grave.

CAROL. So I can find it

BARBARA. Look at that cloud
Look at that big black cloud
That was an ugly storm wasn't it?

CYNTHIA. I wonder how many people died

CAROL. I have no idea

GABRIEL. It's kinda feels like the end of the world doesn't it?

BARBARA. It's just so balmy

GABRIEL. It'd be kinda fun if it were really the end of the world. If it were really, really the end, and we were the very last humans on earth and we got to see it all end? Carol? Like when Pioneer Junior High became Pioneer Middle School. Remember, Carol? When the Junior High became a Middle School and we were the very last class of 9th graders at Pioneer? Carol?

KAYDEN. I dropped my cookie

BARBARA. Well pick it up

GABRIEL. Hi honey

CAROL. Hi

GABRIEL. How's my baby?

CAROL. Quiet. Not kicking

GABRIEL. I mean my other baby. Come here. I want to give you a kiss

CAROL. In a minute

GABRIEL. Kiss kiss

CAROL. In a minute, Gabriel. Jesus

> *A huge gust of wind.*

GABRIEL.
We are in the
tornado
We are in the
tornado!

CAROL.
Weeeeee! It's
fun isn't it.
Hold on to
me. Hold on
to me

CYNTHIA.
Whoa! I lost
my balance.

BARBARA.
If you get
scared
Kayden
just cry out
one word.
JESUS. Just
as loud as
you can.
That's the
only word
you need.

KAYDEN.
I can't
breathe
I can't
breathe

This wind
is literally
pushing me
over. It's
pushing me
over. Oh
my god. It's
pushing me
over.

Grab my
hand. Grab
my hand.
I'll help you
up. Grab my
hand

Wheeeeee!
Wheeee! It's
fun, see?

The wind stops.

GABRIEL. Come on let's get back to the car before it starts
up again

CAROL. I'm giddy. I'm giddy after that

GABRIEL. Hurry, hurry. / Back to the car folks

CYNTHIA. It *is* late isn't it? Wow. I could use some breakfast

BARBARA. We are not leaving until you pick that cookie up off the ground, Kayden

> *Kayden bends down to pick up the cookie*

KAYDEN. It's wet

CAROL. Come on, Kayden. Just leave the cookie

> *Gabriel scoops Kayden up and holds her high above his head.*

GABRIEL. Hi girl. How's my kiddo?

> *A huge crack. A giant tree falls on top of Gabriel and Kayden.*

CAROL. Oh my god

> *Long silence.*

BARBARA. Jesus

Jesus

> *The lights shift and the forest evaporates. Carol and Cynthia once again stand in front of the wrecked house. It's utterly destroyed. The barricade of furniture is still there – a jumbled pile of beds, chairs, lamps… The women survey the wreckage.*

CAROL. Well

CYNTHIA. Well

CAROL. There it is. Just how we left it

CYNTHIA. Hi house

> *They look at the house.*

CYNTHIA. Are you okay? Do you want some water?

> *Carol doesn't answer.*

CYNTHIA. You can clean it up

Save a lot of it, I bet

CAROL. Uh-huh

> *Carol picks her way into the pile of stuff.*

CYNTHIA. Carol what are you doing?

CAROL. Here's my lamp
  And my table

> *Carol disappears into the pile.*

CYNTHIA. Carol be careful!

CAROL. And my carpet!
  And my egg beaters!
  And my bathrobe.

> *Carol finds something.*

CAROL. *Oh…*

CYNTHIA. Carol
  I need to go soon
  I need to head back over the pass before its dark

> *Carol reappears from the pile.*

CYNTHIA. I'm sorry

> *Carol tosses a plastic grocery sack to Cynthia.*

CAROL. That's for you

CYNTHIA. What is it?

CAROL. It's from Gabriel

CYNTHIA. Oh my god

CAROL. I want you to have it

> *Cynthia opens the plastic grocery sack and delicately pulls out the beige tunic.*

CYNTHIA. It's pretty. It's so, so pretty. Don't you think it's pretty?

CAROL. Put it on

> *Cynthia pulls on the beige tunic over her clothes.*

CYNTHIA. Oh my god. Carol. I love it. I really love it

CAROL. It looks nice on you

CYNTHIA. It really does, doesn't it?

CAROL. It looks really, really nice

They look at each other. It's sad, generous, warm, impossibly distant. Cynthia in the tunic. Carol sitting on top of the pile.

CAROL. You should go

CYNTHIA. I can stay

CAROL. You don't have to stay

CYNTHIA. I can stay for like 15 more minutes
> *(beat)*
15 more minutes and then I'll go

> *Barbara appears in the distance.*

BARBARA. Carol! I found our roof. It's up in a tree! I found our roof!
> *It starts to rain.*

End

Printed in the USA
CPSIA information can be obtained
at www.ICGtesting.com
LVHW010601300923
759618LV00044B/1204